JAMES
FARMER

and the
Freedom Rides

Robert E. Jakoubek

GATEWAY CIVIL RIGHTS
THE MILLBROOK PRESS
BROOKFIELD, CONNECTICUT

Library of Congress Cataloging-in-Publication Data
Jakoubek, Robert E.
James Farmer and the freedom rides / Robert E. Jakoubek.
p.   cm.—(Gateway civil rights)
Includes bibliographical references and index.
Summary: Presents the life and times of the black civil rights activist who formed CORE and organized the Freedom Rides.
ISBN 1-56294-381-2 (lib. bdg.)
1. Farmer, James, 1920- —Juvenile literature. 2. Afro-Americans—Biography—Juvenile literature. 3. Civil rights workers—United States—Biography—Juvenile literature. 4. Afro-Americans—Civil rights—Southern States—Juvenile literature. 5. Civil rights movement—Southern States—History—20th century—Juvenile literature. [1. Farmer, James, 1920- . 2. Civil rights workers. 3. Afro-Americans—Biography. 4. Civil rights movements—History.] I. Title. II. Series.
E185.97.F37J35 1994
323′.092—dc20   [B]   93-24143   CIP   AC

Photographs courtesy of Wide World Photos: cover, pp. 10, 20, 28; Black Star: pp. 1 (Sven Simon), 4 (Marvin Hardee), 14 (Flip Schulke), 29 (Will McBride); UPI/Bettmann: cover inset, pp. 2–3, 16, 21, 22, 25, 27, 30–31; Mississippi Department of Archives and History: p. 7; Schomburg Center for Research in Black Culture, New York Public Library: pp. 8, 19.

Published by The Millbrook Press
2 Old New Milford Road, Brookfield, Connecticut 06804

The Trailways bus carrying the Freedom Riders arrives in Jackson, Mississippi, on May 24, 1961.

It was a blazing hot day in Holly Springs, Mississippi. Three-year-old James Farmer was thirsty. "Mommy, I want a Coke," he said, looking up at his mother.

Pearl Farmer hesitated. She saw that her son had his eye on the drugstore across the street. Sadly, she had to tell her son that he could not be served at the store's soda fountain. Why not? James wanted to know.

"You're colored," his mother said.

James lost his taste for a Coke. He and his mother walked home in silence. When they got there, Pearl Farmer went to her bedroom, threw herself across the bed, and began to cry. James's father came and sat by his son. He did not say a word.

At the tender age of three, James had learned the most bitter of life's lessons. Because he was black he would have to endure the system of racial segregation.

Throughout the American South segregation was the law of the land. When African Americans traveled, they passed through bus and train stations with separate "colored" waiting rooms, water fountains, and toilets. They rode in separate railway coaches or in seats at the backs of buses. Blacks attended separate schools. They were barred from hotels and restaurants where whites slept and ate. They were denied entry to all the famous southern universities. Only with great difficulty could African Americans register to vote in elections.

It was no wonder that Pearl Farmer came home and cried for her son and the painful lesson he had just learned.

"They'll Have to Kill Me"

James Leonard Farmer, Jr., was born on January 12, 1920, in Marshall, Texas, a town where his father was the minister of a Methodist church. The elder Farmer—J. Leonard, as everyone called him—was a remarkable man. As a boy, young James watched with wonder as his father sat under a tree outside their house reading books written in Latin, Greek, French, German, and Arabic. A man dedicated to learning, J. Leonard Farmer had been the first African American to earn the degree of Doctor of Philosophy (Ph.D.) in the state of Texas.

A few years after James's birth, the Farmers moved from Marshall to Holly Springs, Mississippi, where J. Leonard taught at Rust College, a black institution. A few years later, Farmer took his family back to Texas. In Austin, the state capital, Farmer secured a position as professor of religion and philosophy at Samuel Houston College, another black school.

The Farmers lived a pleasant life in Austin. Although they were a long way from being wealthy, they had more than most. Best of all, shortly after they moved there, J. Leonard was able

James Farmer's father was an exceptionally well-educated man who taught at Rust College, a black institution in Holly Springs, Mississippi.

to buy a car—a big, boxy 1927 Dodge. On Sundays, after church, J. Leonard would pile his family into the Dodge and take them on long drives through the hilly countryside outside Austin.

On one of these drives, J. Leonard accidentally hit a pig that had strayed into the road. He drove on. "Don't you think you should have stopped?" Pearl Farmer asked.

"No," J. Leonard said firmly. "Out in these rural parts, Negroes are killed for less."

Down the road he pulled over to a shady spot where his wife and children spread a blanket and brought out a picnic lunch of fried chicken and lemonade. Their meal was soon interrupted. A black pickup truck screeched to a stop beside the Dodge and two angry white men rushed toward them. One carried a shotgun. He announced that it was his pig Farmer had hit. "You done killed my hog, nigger," he yelled. "You're gonna pay a pretty penny for that hog."

Even public beaches were segregated during James's childhood.

Holding his straw hat in his hands, casting his eyes downward, J. Leonard said he was sorry. He would pay for the dead animal. "How much do you want for it?" he asked. "Forty-five dollars," said the man. J. Leonard silently handed them his most recent paycheck from the college, fifty-seven dollars for two weeks' work.

Deliberately, the white man let the check slip through his fingers. "Pick it up, nigger," he sneered.

Young James was watching every move. "Everything in me," he recalled years later, "silently screamed, 'Don't do it, Daddy. Don't pick it up. He dropped it. Let him pick it up.'"

J. Leonard quickly bent over and retrieved the check.

James could not bear to see his father humiliated like that. "I was overwhelmed with anger," he remembered. "I turned and walked back to the patch of shade and sat down. I was silent, but I thought, 'I'll never do that when I grow up. They'll have to kill me.' "

"The Key"

Taking after his father, young James was a bright boy and a quick learner. By the time he entered the first grade, he already knew his numbers and how to read and write. When he was twelve he won a series of high school speech contests. At fourteen he was ready for college. In the fall of 1934 he enrolled as a freshman at Wiley College in Marshall, Texas.

James Farmer breezed through his courses at Wiley. All the while, he was thinking about what he was going to do with his life after college. More than anything else he wanted to find a way to fight the system of segregation that every day humiliated him, his father, his family, and all other African Americans. "My ambition was to wage war on racism," he recalled, "but how would I earn a living?"

He decided on the ministry. In 1938, after graduating from Wiley, Farmer left Texas for Washington, D.C., and Howard University. At Howard, one of the country's most distinguished black universities, he would study for the clergy.

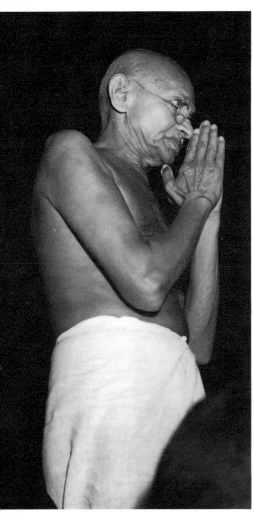

James Farmer believed that Mohandas Gandhi's nonviolent approach to protest could be used in the United States to bring about an end to racism.

While at Howard, James Farmer learned about the life and work of Mohandas K. Gandhi, the leader of the struggle to end British rule in India. Gandhi insisted that any action or protest against the British government be nonviolent. He organized Indians into a mass movement that peacefully demonstrated for independence from Great Britain.

Farmer came to believe that Gandhi's tactics might work to end segregation in the United States. He envisioned massive, peaceful protests against racism. Nonviolence was essential. "Like Gandhi's army," Farmer recalled thinking, "it must be nonviolent. . . . Yes, Gandhi has the key for me to unlock the door to the American dream." For Farmer, the American dream meant equality for African Americans.

Farmer got together with other Howard students who thought the same way. He became active in the Fellowship of Reconciliation, or FOR, an organization committed to achieving social change through nonviolence. Believing that all wars were wrong, Farmer spoke out against America's entry into World War II. On one occasion, in early 1941, he was invited to the White House. Part of a delegation of young people, Farmer boldly expressed his anti-war views to President Franklin D. Roosevelt.

In the classroom Farmer studied the connections between religion and racism. Too often, he concluded, churches were guilty of prejudice and discrimination. In May 1941, upon his graduation from Howard, he made a big decision. He would not become a minister after all. The Methodist Church, of which he was a member, was segregated. "I did not see how I could honestly preach the gospel of Christ in a church that practiced discrimination," he would say years later.

He would continue the struggle for equality in other ways.

Into the Fray

After graduating from divinity school at Howard, Farmer took a job with the Fellowship of Reconciliation for fifteen dollars a week. FOR sent him throughout the country to make anti-war speeches.

While working out of the FOR office in Chicago, Farmer saw that racial prejudice was not limited to the South. To be sure, northern cities like Chicago did not have formal laws upholding segregation. But, in practice, Chicago was every bit as segregated as southern states and towns. African Americans were forced to live in segregated neighborhoods and were kept out of restaurants and stores that served whites.

Feeling the need to challenge both northern and southern segregation, Farmer and several others from FOR met in Chicago in April 1942. They founded a new organization, the Committee of Racial Equality, or CORE. With both black and white members, CORE planned to use the nonviolent tactics of Gandhi to confront American racism. The small new organization elected Farmer its leader. Soon, FOR members were organizing CORE chapters in cities across the country, and in June 1943 the organization held its first national meeting. Farmer, its national chairman, called for ''interracial, nonviolent direct action'' against segregation.

As chairman of CORE, Farmer directed several successful protests, most notably against restaurants in Chicago that refused service to blacks. The organization steadily gained more members. In 1944, reflecting its larger following, it changed its name to the Congress of Racial Equality.

Despite his successes, Farmer's days with CORE were numbered. He kept having trouble with others in the organization, particularly those who had stayed loyal to the FOR group. They often opposed Farmer's ideas for massive protests. In 1944,

Farmer put an end to the bickering among the top leaders of CORE by resigning as its national director. For the next seventeen years CORE would continue without him.

Beliefs into Practice

Between 1944 and 1961, Farmer's commitment to equality, social justice, and nonviolence remained as strong as ever. It was, however, hard for him to find a position where he could put his beliefs into practice. For a long while after leaving CORE, he worked as an organizer for labor unions. Then, in 1959, he returned to the civil rights movement by taking a job as program director at the National Association for the Advancement of Colored People (NAACP), the nation's oldest and largest civil rights organization.

Farmer was glad to be back working for the rights of black Americans. It was an exciting time. In 1954 the Supreme Court of the United States had declared that racial segregation in public schools was illegal. A year later, Martin Luther King, Jr., a young, courageous, and eloquent Baptist minister in Montgomery, Alabama, led a successful campaign to end segregation in the Montgomery bus system. Throughout the South, more and more African Americans were resisting segregation by following King's example of nonviolent protest.

MARTIN LUTHER KING, JR.

In 1955, Martin Luther King, Jr., was the twenty-six-year-old pastor of the Dexter Avenue Baptist Church in Montgomery, Alabama. Reluctantly, he assumed the leadership of Montgomery's blacks in their effort to end segregation on the city's buses. For a year he directed a boycott that successfully kept black riders off the buses. Eventually, the Supreme Court of the United States declared the segregation laws of Alabama illegal.

The Montgomery Bus Boycott established King as the nation's premier black leader. Over the next twelve years, from 1957 until his assassination in 1968, King bravely fought racism and discrimination. It was a frightening, bitter battle. In the streets of southern towns and on the sidewalks of northern cities, King and his followers were beaten, arrested, and jailed. Their homes and churches were burned, their families threatened, their friends and allies murdered. But, in the end, they awakened the world to the shame of racism in America.

Like James Farmer, King held an unshakable belief in nonviolence. And, like Farmer, King had been greatly influenced by the teachings of Gandhi. In 1964, King was awarded the Nobel Peace Prize, one of the highest honors in the world. "Nonviolence," he said accepting the prize, "is the answer to the crucial political and moral questions of our time—the need for man to overcome oppression and violence without resorting to violence and oppression."

In 1954 the Supreme Court ruled that racial segregation in public schools was illegal. The winning attorneys who argued the case were, from left to right, George E. C. Hayes, Thurgood Marshall, and James Nabrit, Jr.

But the NAACP preferred not to get involved in campaigns of nonviolent protest. Its great work had been done in the nation's courtrooms, where its lawyers had won momentous victories in civil rights cases. At the NAACP, Farmer felt frustrated, like a football player stuck on the sidelines.

In early 1961, CORE, the organization that Farmer had helped establish, was looking for a national director. CORE still staged nonviolent protests against segregation, but, over the years, it had not always been effective. It had little money, a small membership, and it got almost no attention from the press. A new national director, it was hoped, would breathe life into the organization and get CORE into the thick of the battle for civil rights.

CORE first tried to recruit Martin Luther King, Jr. He politely turned down the offer. They next turned to the NAACP's program director. James Farmer jumped at the chance to return to CORE. On February 1, 1961, he became the organization's national director.

"Creating a Crisis"

In December 1960 the U.S. Supreme Court outlawed racial segregation in train stations and bus terminals. For the most part, the South acted as if it had never heard of the decision. Southern stations and terminals remained as segregated as ever. Nearly all contained two waiting rooms—one for whites, another for "coloreds."

Farmer and CORE decided to challenge this continued segregation. On March 13, 1961, Farmer called for volunteers to conduct Freedom Rides through the South. Traveling by bus, the CORE riders would deliberately ignore the "whites only" and "colored" signs in the waiting rooms, restaurants, and restrooms of southern bus stations.

By going into the Deep South and ignoring segregation, Farmer and the Freedom Riders were asking for trouble. But trouble would draw attention to their cause. And trouble might get the federal government to take a more active role in the struggle against segregation. "We planned the Freedom Ride with the specific intention of creating a crisis," he recalled. "We were counting on the bigots in the South to do our work for us. We figured that the government would have to respond if we created a situation that was headline news all over the world."

On May 4, 1961, in Washington, D.C., thirteen Freedom Riders—seven blacks and six whites—split into two groups. Both groups contained blacks and whites. One boarded a Trailways bus. The other got on a Greyhound. Slowly, they made their way south, first to Virginia, then into North Carolina. They meant to travel all the way to New Orleans.

At first the Freedom Riders did not encounter any difficulty. Some terminals had even taken down the "whites" and "colored" signs before they arrived. But as they got into the Deep South, Farmer recalled, "we began to taste southern hate."

Southern bus and train stations continued to ignore the Supreme Court's 1960 ruling that outlawed racial segregation in waiting rooms.

COLORED
WAITING ROOM

On May 14, 1961, the Greyhound bus was set on fire by a white mob outside of Anniston, Alabama. People all around the country were shocked by the hatred and violence directed at the Freedom Riders.

On May 14, Mother's Day, the Greyhound bus carrying the CORE riders rolled into Anniston, Alabama. A white mob attacked. Armed with clubs and iron bars, the mob smashed windows and slashed tires. Outside of town, the mob attacked a second time and set the bus on fire. As the terrified riders staggered out the door of the burning bus, white hoodlums punched, beat, and kicked them.

The Trailways bus made it to Birmingham, Alabama's largest city. A gang of forty whites were waiting on the platform. The local police had told the whites that they could have fifteen minutes to do as they pleased. In that quarter hour, the white mob boarded the bus and attacked the riders with lead pipes, baseball bats, and tire chains.

The bloodbath in Alabama was worse than anything Farmer had expected. In Birmingham, CORE called off the Freedom Ride.

Farmer himself was in deep sorrow. On May 13, the day before the riders reached Alabama, his father had died in Washington, D.C. He had left the riders to attend the funeral. By tele-

A furious gang of whites attacks a white Freedom Rider in Birmingham, Alabama, during the Freedom Riders' stop there to protest racial segregation on buses.

phone, he heard of the savage assaults in Alabama. He agreed that CORE should cancel the remainder of the journey. He also permitted another civil rights organization, the Student Nonviolent Coordinating Committee (SNCC, pronounced "snick") to take up where CORE was leaving off.

On the second leg of their trip, the Freedom Riders prepare to leave Montgomery, Alabama, under heavy guard by state troopers and National Guardsmen.

"Bigotry's Main Den"

After his father's funeral, Farmer flew to Montgomery, Alabama. There, organizers for SNCC were preparing to continue the Freedom Ride into Mississippi and Louisiana. When Farmer arrived, Montgomery was on the verge of a riot. At a mass meeting in a black church, he and Martin Luther King, Jr., spoke to more than a thousand African Americans, all of them angry and frightened by the violence against the Freedom Riders. As the meeting progressed, a white mob gathered outside and surrounded the church. But the mob did not attack. Federal marshals and units of the National Guard were protecting the church.

The presence of these marshals and of the National Guard meant that the federal government at long last had intervened. Attorney General Robert F. Kennedy was keeping a close watch on the events in Alabama. This attention, of course, was what Farmer had wanted all along. The Freedom Ride's purpose was to get the federal government involved on the side of the foes of segregation.

The eyes of the world were on Alabama and the Freedom Ride. A photograph of the flaming Greyhound bus in Anniston had been on the front pages of newspapers everywhere. And everywhere people had been shocked by the savage violence.

On May 24 the Freedom Ride started off again, heading from Montgomery to Mississippi, the state that Farmer called "bigotry's main den." At first, Farmer had mixed feelings about going along. It was now really a SNCC operation, and he had work to do at the CORE office. But then a young woman who was boarding the bus pleaded, "Jim, *please.*"

"Get my luggage out of the car and put it on the bus," he said. With that he joined the riders.

When they reached Jackson, Mississippi, Farmer led the riders off the bus and into the terminal. Arm in arm with another rider, he strode into the whites-only waiting room and then walked toward the whites-only restaurant. In the doorway, the Jackson chief of police told him not to enter. When Farmer and the other riders refused to move on, they were all arrested. They had violated the local segregation laws.

Attorney General Kennedy figured that the riders would be in jail just a short time. He had arranged with Mississippi officials to have them released if they paid a small fine.

But Farmer and the Freedom Riders would have nothing to do with Kennedy's arrangement. Farmer announced that they would all go to jail rather than admit their guilt by paying a fine for breaking an unjust law. In his struggle for Indian Independence, Gandhi had often gone to jail. Farmer was now proud to do what his idol had done.

For the next six weeks, Farmer and the Freedom Riders stayed in the cramped and dirty cells of Mississippi prisons.

James Farmer, shown here walking from the Jackson police station to a waiting "paddy wagon," held his head high as he was arrested along with fourteen others for refusing to leave a whites-only restaurant.

They ate miserable, tasteless food. They seldom saw the light of day. Worst of all, they faced the threats and insults of white prison guards. On July 7, Farmer was released. He returned to New York to a hero's welcome at CORE headquarters.

Meanwhile, the Freedom Rides rolled on. By the end of the summer of 1961, more than a thousand people had taken part. The federal government was forced to act. Robert Kennedy issued instructions to federal agencies to begin enforcing the Supreme Court's ban on segregation in bus and train stations. It took a while, but by the end of 1962, separate facilities for whites and blacks were a thing of the past.

A Crusader for Freedom

The Freedom Ride established CORE as one of the country's major civil rights organizations. Under Farmer's leadership, CORE gained new members, new contributions, and new attention.

"We have to continue to create crises like the Freedom Ride," he said. True to his word, Farmer's CORE waged many battles. It fought for desegregated restaurants along southern highways and spearheaded campaigns to register black voters.

Black and white demonstrators gather in front of the Lincoln Memorial during the March on Washington for Jobs and Freedom in 1963.

In 1963, Farmer helped organize the massive March on Washington for Jobs and Freedom. Labor unions that were slow to enroll blacks also felt the sting of CORE's protest. Within black neighborhoods, CORE sponsored programs for better housing and better education.

In January 1966, after five years, Farmer stepped down as national director at CORE. At first he turned to politics, running unsuccessfully for Congress in 1968. In 1969, President Richard M. Nixon appointed him assistant secretary of the Department of Health, Education, and Welfare. But helping direct an enormous government agency did not suit him, and he resigned the following year.

What did suit him was teaching. In 1985, Farmer became a history professor at Mary Washington College in Fredericksburg, Virginia. In his classroom, students learned about the civil rights movement and heard firsthand accounts of Farmer's own crusade for peace, justice, and human dignity.

After his resignation from CORE and a brief time in politics, James Farmer found great satisfaction in teaching. Here he conducts a class at Mary Washington College in 1990 on the history of the civil rights movement.

IMPORTANT DATES IN THE LIFE OF JAMES FARMER

1920   James Leonard Farmer, Jr., is born on January 12 in Marshall, Texas.

1941   Farmer graduates from divinity school at Howard University.

1942   Farmer and others create the Committee of Racial Equality (CORE). Farmer becomes its national chairman.

1944   Farmer steps down as head of CORE.

1959   Farmer becomes program director at the NAACP.

1961   Farmer again serves as CORE's national director. He organizes the Freedom Rides to challenge segregation in the South. On May 24, Farmer and other riders are arrested in Jackson, Mississippi.

1966   Farmer steps down as leader of CORE.

1969   President Richard M. Nixon appoints Farmer assistant secretary of the Department of Health, Education, and Welfare. Farmer resigns the following year.

1985   Farmer is appointed professor of history at Mary Washington College in Fredericksburg, Virginia.

FIND OUT MORE ABOUT JAMES FARMER AND HIS TIMES

The Civil Rights Movement in America from 1865 to the Present by Patricia and Fredrick McKissack (Chicago: Childrens Press, 1987).

James Farmer by Jeff Sklansky (New York: Chelsea House Publishers, 1992).

Martin Luther King, Jr., and the March Toward Freedom by Rita Hakim (Brookfield, Conn.: The Millbrook Press, 1991).

The Year They Walked: Rosa Parks and the Montgomery Bus Boycott by Beatrice Siegel (New York: Macmillan, 1992).

INDEX

Page numbers in *italics* refer to illustrations.